M000275231

...se your voice."

Roxann Biesack

Millie Mae Speaks Up to a Bully Today

Roxann Biesack

Copyright © 2015 Roxann Biesack.

All rights reserved. No part of this book may be used or reproduced by any means, graphic, electronic, or mechanical, including photocopying, recording, taping or by any information storage retrieval system without the written permission of the author except in the case of brief quotations embodied in critical articles and reviews.

LifeRich Publishing is a registered trademark of The Reader's Digest Association, Inc.

LifeRich Publishing books may be ordered through booksellers or by contacting:

LifeRich Publishing
1663 Liberty Drive
Bloomington, IN 47403
www.liferichpublishing.com
1 (888) 238-8637

Because of the dynamic nature of the Internet, any web addresses or links contained in this book may have changed since publication and may no longer be valid. The views expressed in this work are solely those of the author and do not necessarily reflect the views of the publisher, and the publisher hereby disclaims any responsibility for them.

Any people depicted in stock imagery provided by Thinkstock are models, and such images are being used for illustrative purposes only.
Certain stock imagery © Thinkstock.

ISBN: 978-1-4897-0516-7 (sc)
ISBN: 978-1-4897-0518-1 (hc)
ISBN: 978-1-4897-0517-4 (e)

Print information available on the last page.

LifeRich Publishing rev. date: 09/04/2015

I can recommend this manuscript because it teaches children a positive approach in confronting a person who is bullying them. The story is appealing to young children. "Squeaky" is an enjoyable character. Children love stories with animals that talk. The emphasis on speaking up when you are being hurt is important. Young children often are afraid and don't know what to say so they become victimized more. This story clearly shows a girl who learned how speaking up helped her deal with the problem she was having.

Parents and teachers need good literature that assist them in helping young children understand who a bully is and what to do if you are bullied. Throughout the course of a school year, a teacher looks for books that reinforce good behaviors. This book would be of value in the classroom.

Five and six year olds are just starting to understand the concept of children who bully. This story gives them a simple and meaningful introduction to bullying.

Seven and eight year olds would be able to read this story. They could act out the story if it were made into a short class play. They also could write their own story when they had to speak up to someone who was bullying them or a friend.

At this time, there is a lot of attention in schools regarding bullying... anti bullying pledges, etc. The schools are very serious in their quest to successfully make children aware of bullying. The goal is to provide a safe and healthy environment for all the children.

Rosemary Cicero

Rosemary is a retired teacher, with thirty plus years in early childhood classrooms.

I recommend this manuscript because it teaches a wonderful message and is engaging. I had a hard time putting the manuscript down and wanted to keep on reading. The story is realistic and represents what many students and children go through at school. I liked how Millie Mae had normal reactions to her problem with the bully. I also thought that the idea of having an animal (tree frog) as a friend was great. Children love stories with animals in them. The way Squeaky and Millie Mae talked through her problem with Sally Ann, was a great model for how children could talk and think through problems with others. Speaking up for yourself in an appropriate way is a life skill that is needed and some children need to be taught. This book would be a great story to read and a teaching tool as well.

This book would be of interest through most elementary grades. There are few books out there that address this topic in such an appropriate way, yet still have a page turner of a story.

Deidre Olson

Deidre has been an elementary librarian for fourteen years, and is the mother of two children.

I dedicate this book to my mother, who waited patiently to see this book published, and who never said an unkind word about anyone.

Bella Boo and I walked home from school together, as usual, that day. We were quiet. I could tell she wanted to talk to me, but didn't know what to say. I didn't either. She fidgeted with her back pack, ate a cookie that was left in her lunch box, and jumped over every crack in the sidewalk. From my driveway, I watched Bella Boo skip to her house. When I couldn't see her anymore, I ran to the tree outside my bedroom window. I had to talk to Squeaky! As I climbed the tree to my favorite spot, I felt a lump in my throat. It was so quiet up there, and with all of the leaves around me, I felt safe; like nobody could see me.

"Maybe I should try to get rid of this lump in my throat before I talk to Squeaky," I thought. Instead, I heard myself whisper, "Squeaky, where are you? I need to talk to you!" I waited. The leaves started to rustle above me. The rustling got closer and closer, and then my little tree frog friend landed on the branch next to me.

"What's wrong, Millie Mae?" he asked gently. "Usually you're so happy when you get home from school. Did something happen today?" As much as I wanted to tell Squeaky, I couldn't talk. My throat felt so tight. "Millie?" he prodded, "I've never known you to be so quiet...what happened in school...

"There's a FROG in my throat, ok," I blurted! I was surprised at my anger.

"That's not funny, Millie Mae." Squeaky was still gentle, though. He stared at me, waiting. I looked away so he wouldn't see the tears in my eyes.

"I'm sorry, Squeaky. You're right, that wasn't funny." I cleared my throat and was determined to tell Squeaky about mean Sally Ann. "I hate Sally Ann, Squeaky! She's a BULLY!" Squeaky waited patiently to hear more. That's the thing about Squeaky; he listens to me, even when I say some things I'm not supposed to say, like, "I hate someone."

"Ok, Squeaky," I cleared my throat, feeling words ready to come out. "Sally Ann wouldn't let me play basketball with her and the other kids at recess. She even let Bella Boo play, but not me!"

"Did you ask her why, Millie Mae?" Squeaky blinked sadly. "Why wouldn't she let you play today?"

"No, but I told her I didn't want to play anyway, and I ran to the tire swing."

"Good, Millie. Sometimes you have to walk away when someone is being mean."

"That's just it Squeak, when I ran to the tire swing, Sally Ann ran after me. She pushed me down and told me I couldn't play with anyone or on anything all recess. Bella Boo stayed with me when I fell," I said softly.

Squeaky's red eyes got big. "Did you get hurt?" We both looked down at my hands. They were dirty, and scraped and red. My cheeks felt red too, and hot. I had more to tell Squeaky.

"I told her she wasn't the boss of me! She didn't listen! She pushed me down again and punched me on my arm!" I looked away from Squeaky again, trying to hide the tears.

But the tears went away when Squeaky asked, "Has Sally Ann ever been mean to you before?" I broke a small branch off the tree!

"Yes!" I knew the tree I was sitting in was Squeaky's home, but I couldn't seem to control myself. I threw the branch and looked back at him. "She tripped me once at recess!" I wanted to break another branch!

"Anything else, Millie?"

"Everyone laughed! I felt stupid! Why, Squeaky? Why is she so mean to me? I never did anything bad to her!"

Squeaky was quiet for a while. He rubbed his eyes, blinked like he was going to cry, but then he said, "It's not anything you've ever said to Sally Ann. It's not about who you are, or what you look like or anything you did or didn't do."

"Then why Squeaky, I don't understand?"

"Because," he said so quietly, "she thinks she can." Squeaky closed his eyes. He was quiet for so long, I thought he had fallen asleep. Just as I was about to climb down, he croaked, "Millie!" so loudly, I almost fell out of the tree! "So Millie, what are you going to do tomorrow if Sally Ann is mean to you again?"

"Punch her in that mean mouth of hers!" My mind was made up!

"Hmmm...ok Millie...any better ideas?"

"Sure," I said, "I could kick her!"

"Hmmm...ok Millie, I know you're angry and you want to hurt her too. But what if you punch her and kick her and she punches you and kicks you harder?"

"I'm not afraid of her! I'm not afraid of her! I'm not afraid..." each time I said that to Squeaky, I realized, I was afraid. I closed my eyes and thought for a long time, but I couldn't figure out what I should do if Sally Ann is mean again. "I don't know Squeaky. Tell me what to do."

"Well, I have some ideas you can try."

"Pull her hair!" I knew I was wrong.

Squeaky jumped and sat on my shoulder. He nestled into my red shirt and said, "No Millie, when she comes toward you on the playground, **SPEAK UP!** Say, leave me alone Sally Ann. I'm not afraid of you! Say it loud, just like you said it to me."

"And what if she still comes after me?"

"Tell an adult right away. Will you try this tomorrow, Millie Mae?"

Climbing down the tree, I wasn't feeling like Squeaky really helped me. But I did feel better about finally telling him what was going on with Sally Ann. I thought he was going to think I was stupid because I let someone bully me. I thought it was my fault. Squeaky listened to me and didn't laugh at me. Maybe I could try his suggestions.

When I jumped out of the tree, he had one last suggestion that I wasn't too sure about.

"Millie Mae, wear your red sweater and your earmuffs tomorrow."

"What? It's not cold enough to wear earmuffs! I'll look silly! Do you want me to get beat up again?"

"Just wear them, Millie Mae. For once, don't ask questions and do as I say."

I shook my head, muttered, "EARMUFFS", and went into my house.

I wore my sweater the next day, and my earmuffs, like Squeaky said to do. It felt silly, but there was something about Squeaky's voice, that made me listen to him. During spelling class, Ms. Pearl called on me to use our new spelling word, 'nobody' in a sentence. Sally Ann spun around in her seat and stared at me. She looked so mean!

"Um," I stared at the word, but my stomach felt sick and my hands were shaking. I put them in my sweater pockets so no one could see them shake. There he was! Squeaky was in my right pocket! He wrapped around my finger, like a big hug. "Squeak...I mean..."

"Millie Mae, are you ok?" Ms. Pearl was suspicious.

"Yes, Ms. Pearl!" I felt a little stronger. I looked at the word on the black board again.

"You can do it", whispered Squeaky.

"Nobody is allowed to hurt me!" I said, and I stared back at Sally Ann, **"NOBODY!"** I sat down at my desk, feeling very brave!

Bella walked extra close to me during recess. I kept my hand in my sweater pocket. Squeaky hugged my finger and croaked very quietly, "It's normal to be afraid, Millie. Wherever I am, in my tree, or in your pocket, I am always with you," he whispered. "Now go play with Sally Ann." As he squeaked, almost silently in my pocket, his words kept repeating in my mind; "It's normal to be afraid-it's normal to be afraid." But someone else's voice shouted over it!

"Look at those silly earmuffs!" Sally Ann started chanting. "Millie Mae is wearing red earmuffs today! Look at Millie Mae, she is wearing red earmuffs today!" The other kids stopped playing basketball and started laughing and chanting with Sally Ann. Bella Boo stared at me, as I felt my face get as red as my stupid earmuffs. I felt helpless, as Bella ran toward one of the teachers on the playground. Where was Squeaky now, when I really needed him? I dug deeper into my pocket, but Squeaky was gone!

What did Squeaky tell me to do, and where is he? Suddenly, I heard him! He had hopped his way up my sweater and was hiding under my right earmuff, and he was hissing into my ear!

"Say it again, Millie, just like you did in class!"

I tried but only stammered, "no-no-nobody is allowed to hurt me." Sally Ann crossed her arms and it seemed like everyone was laughing. Everyone, except this one kid. He just kept bouncing the basketball and watching. He wasn't laughing at me.

"Say it!" croaked Squeaky.

"NOBODY IS ALLOWED TO HURT ME!" I heard myself get louder! "NOT EVEN YOU SALLY ANN! YOU'RE JUST MEAN!"

Everyone was quiet.

"She's right, Sally Ann, you are acting mean." It was the boy with the basketball. He turned to me, "Hi, I'm Greg. You can play with us." He threw the ball to me, shouting, "Make a shot, Millie Mae!"

"Just have fun," Squeaky chimed in my ear. I was surprised to see the ball go through the net!

Sally was sitting alone by the fence. I was having too much fun to wonder why Bell Boo sat next to her, or to even wonder what they were talking about. When the bell rang, I made sure Squeaky was back in my pocket, before I took my earmuffs off. It was the best recess ever, but I was wondering where my friend, Bella, was. As we walked into class, I saw her walking in with Sally Ann. Somehow, Sally didn't look mean anymore. She looked just like the other kids walking to their seats, in our classroom.

Walking home from school, I couldn't wait to ask Bella Boo why she was talking to mean, Sally Ann.

"She's really not so mean, Millie." I waited, curious to find out how pushing me down, hitting me, and not letting me play at recess, was NOT mean! Bella seemed to know what I was thinking. "I know how she treated you, Millie, was mean. She acts that way because she's sad."

I kept thinking about how normal Sally looked after I spoke up for myself; how she just left the group and sat by the fence. So I looked at Bella, and listened.

"Her older cousin is living with her until her mom can find a job. She's bigger than Sally Ann and pushes her around a lot. She doesn't let her play with her and Sally's big brother. They call her names and laugh at her all the time."

"So you think Sally treated me the way her cousin treats her?" But when I looked at Bella, I knew she wanted to say more. I said it for her, "and you think we should try to be friends with her, don't you!" Bella Boo just shook her head and skipped toward her house.

When I got home, I climbed the tree to my favorite spot. I remembered how good I felt today when I told Sally Ann that nobody is allowed to hurt me. I gently took Squeaky out of my pocket. He jumped back on to the branch next to me. He looked a little worn out from his long day, in my pocket. He snuggled against a leaf for a while, looking happily at me. Then Squeaky relaxed and closed his eyes.

"Thank you, Squeaky," I whispered, as I started to climb down the tree.

"What are you going to do tomorrow, Millie Mae?" I sat back down and smiled at my little tree frog friend, as he jumped into my lap. The answer seemed easy now. I spoke up for myself today, and I wasn't afraid anymore.

"I'm going to make a new friend tomorrow, Squeaky."

About the author

Roxann Biesack has followed her passion and worked with children for a good portion of her life. She spent three years working with special needs children, including volunteer work with them. As she raised her own children, she ran a licensed daycare, which gave her the opportunity to meet the needs of many different personalities and special needs of individual children. Roxann studied courses for special needs children through the University of Wisconsin Whitewater. Roxann has four adult children, and four grandchildren. She resides in Kenosha, Wisconsin, with her husband.